FREE ADVICE

For information address:
J2B Publishing LLC
4251 Columbia Park Road
Pomdert, MD 20675
www.JBBLLC.com
GladToDoIt@gmail.com

Printed and bonded in the United States of America
The book set in Garamond

ISBN: 978-1-948747-40-0

FREE ADVICE

Richard I. Gold

J2B PUBLISHING

Also By Richard I. Gold

God's Agenda: Religious Poems - Vol. I

Mary's Lamb and other Christmas Poems

God's Love - Easter Poems

Sayings for the Believer

Work is a 4-Letter Word

Dedication

My thanks to my wife who has helped me with the initial review and to those who have reviewed this work over time including my cousin, James Greenlee, and others.

Table of Contents

INTRODUCTION

We all feel compelled to give advice to others about many things whether we know anything about what they are doing or not. Often this advice is off the mark but sometimes it can be something which may be helpful. We should take the advice and consider what wisdom it may contain to help us in our life.

1. FREE ADVICE

When we give advice to others
We think we know best
For we see where they are headed
It is not the way we would bless

Often free advice we get
Is worth what it costs
But we should listen
It may save us from some loss

Advice is advice no matter the cost
So listen and consider
Whether it has an end
Should we take it or dither

Seek the wisdom advice contains
Listen to those who have been there
They may be trying to help us
Or just trying to give us a scare

So weigh your options in life
Look to the end of it all
For by the by and in the end
The future on you doth call

2. THE WISDOM OF THE AGES

The wisdom of the ages
Is written, spoken, and told
From old to young throughout all time
But occasionally from young to old

Wisdom is a beautiful thing
Desirable in every way
When it is something we want
It will help us to find what to do and say

Wisdom can do us no good
If we choose to ignore
No matter how we need it
It will make our good a thing of yore

So listen to the wisdom
Read every word
For when we follow it
The wisdom has been heard

3. ADVICE TO THE YOUNG

When you look at the world
You see many things
Things you want
You hope that happiness will bring

But happiness comes from within
Be content with what you have
More things within your life
Will not fulfillment give

Be not confused
By desire for things
That drain your resources
But destruction may bring

But remember that things
Will weigh you down
When you must make a change
It may not allow you to rebound

Know this in your life:

Know what really matters
You are forever you
Must be your goals in life
A goal that is stable and true

4. MORE ADVICE TO THE YOUNG

You're young, you're strong
You are the future of the earth
But your future
Is what you are worth

The future depends upon you
What future will you get
If you keep what you earn
But lose joy and have to regret

Blaming others is easy
"They did it all to you"
But remember your actions
Are what makes you

This you will remember
When as life you live
You must be ever ready
Answers ready to give

For when you do something
That is how you act
But the consequences are yours
That is a fact

So remember as you live
Responsibility you have
For every word or deed
Are yours forever as you live

5. STILL MORE ADVICE TO THE YOUNG

You're young, you're strong
The future belongs to you
The world is your plum for picking
You know that this is true

You're invincible
Nothing can hurt you
If you fall down
"They" will pick you up, its true

But life is a cruel place
Will take all you have
Give nothing in return
Nothing to save

Go forth to conquer
Go forth to serve
When you reach the end
You'll get what you've earned

6. FOR THE YOUNG OF HEART

For the young of heart
May you find the way
To walk in the right
Not for evil will you have to pay

Your life is not over
Until death comes knocking
You've more to do with your time
Than sit in a chair rocking

For when you're young
Life is your plum
You do whatever you will
Sometimes it's just plain dumb

You can recover
From many mistakes
As long as you try
And have what it takes

7. SOME PLACE ELSE

Someplace else
I'll be great
Someplace else
I'll be good
Someplace else
I'll do what's right
Someplace else
I'll do what I should

In this place
I've done what's common
In this place
I've done what's bad
In this place
I've wronged others
In this place
I've been had

BUT

In some other place
I'd still do the same
In some other place
I'd still be who I am
In some other place
I'd look the same
In some other place
I'd still be me

I can change my location
I can change my car
I can change what I say
But I can't change who I am

8. IT IS GIVEN TO US

It is given to us
To be born once and then to die
We cannot change this
No matter how we try

We have conquered many things
Taken from nature more than we gave
But there is one we cannot conquer
That is the grave

So make the most of your life
Do not take more than you give
Always remember
Do not give up while you live

So live your life for others
Not for yourself alone
Give not up your life
Let your best be known

You must always know
Make life your choice
For death do not volunteer
Give life your voice

For you are not alone
Others love and depend upon you
They have given you so very much
At least to them be true

9. THE QUEST FOR POWER

The quest for power is a human thing
For both great and small
We would make our self gods
With power over all

But if gods were we
Major changes wrought
The world within its orb
Would be brought to naught

Power - is what everyone wants
Power very few have
But wealth and might
Doth responsibility give

10. PROCRASTINATION IS THE THIEF OF TIME

Procrastination is the thief of time
So the sage has told
When we do not do what we should
Deadlines do not hold

We put off many things
Things we do not wish to do
The unpleasant and the hard
These are things that make us true

We should remember
What we must do in life
If we would successful be
Live with little or no strife

11. PROCRASTINATION

When we think of doing things
We think there's plenty of time
To plan, to think, to do
We always want to be in our prime

But the time we have is limited
Only so many hours, so many days
Often it seems
We walk through life in a haze

But putting off
Not doing what we should
Will sap our life of meaning
Keep us from doing good

12. A PERSON WITHOUT HONOR

A person without honor
Is a person who has no name
But all those without honor
Are persons just the same

For honor is the stuff of life
Makes our word worth while
For honor makes our character
Even when we're a child

Whatever we accomplish
Stays with us for life
As we live in this world
We will be judged as we live

13. THERE IS A LINE

There is a line between right and wrong
A line between good and bad
Never cross that fearful line
Cross it and baby you've been had

It is a challenge to knowing what to do
Our instincts we cannot trust
We should be sure of what to do
Before we go for bust

What is right we may know
But doing the right we know
Is a much harder task
This makes life a harder go

14. WALK THE WALK

Walk the walk of life
Talk the talk just so
Long may we live
Before our Maker we know

Long life and good
May it come your way
That you will enjoy yourself
Before that everlasting day

15. THE YOUNG AND THE OLD

The young and the old
Live in the same world
Each doing their own thing
Following their own agenda
Going their way so bold
Their own flags unfurled
When not getting, they bemoan
Their total way to endue
So each marches forth
To do deeds they think are good
But they might consider the end
If the end to know they could

16. THOSE WHO DIED FOR NOTHING

Those who died for nothing
Their death did not count
For they made the decision
To opt out

We all make decisions
To act or not
But if we opt out
The results will be lost

For we know not what is beyond
That everlasting divide
When we make the decision
To cross to the other side

So live your life for others
To do what you know is right
That this is the end
For which we must fight

17. THE WORLD IS A TOUGH PLACE

The world is a tough place
A place of friend and foe
Don't turn your back on anyone
Because you never know

Today's friend
May be tomorrow's foe
Each looking for their own
As through life they go

As for the foes you have
Do not treat them ill
For those you hate today
May be tomorrow's customer

18. THE WORLD IS A TOUGH PLACE II

The world is a tough place
It'll take all you have
Not like they taught you in school
Not what you would give

The world is a tough place
It's tough if you're cunning and smart
But to take the road of stupidity
It'll cut out your very heart

Go forth and do well
Trust only the good
For by having an ally
You'll accomplish all you could

19. SPEND YOUR TIME DOING GOOD

Spend your time doing good
For your fellow man
Give unto others
Work as hard as you can

This is your task
Your task and mine
Create your own biography
Make it great and just

For each of us has an end
A place we must go
Search for the passage to these
In order for you to know

20. DATA IS NOT KNOWLEDGE

Data is not knowledge
Knowledge is more than fact
Data is what we know
Knowledge lets us act

So collect all the facts
Store them one by one
But to make them knowledge
Your job has just begun

Then we find that we get data
About what we've done
The goals we seek
Is the road of life begun

By knowing the facts
By knowing other things
We find the goals we seek
Life will the future bring

21. FIX THE PROBLEM WHEN YOU CAN

Fix the problem when you can
You know that you must proceed
For if the problem is not fixed
You find progress it will impede

The future you will see
When the problems are there
For the problems you have
Is something that others do not care

Each day you face problems
Things that you cannot ignore
When they're too large for you
Seek help before they soar

22. THERE HAS TO BE A BETTER WAY

There has to be a better way
To live upon this earth
Than to see how much we can get
To increase only our girth

What is humankind
To from nature take
This generation is blessed
Future generations must reparations make

Man is the great destroyer
Of nature and of the earth
"Live good, don't worry"
"Nature will heal" is a myth

Where is the passenger pigeon?
The cod are all but gone
The oceans so abundant
Are filled with the stink of man

Hope we are not gone
If we straighten our ways
But to destroy water
Will end our days

23. GETTING AND GIVING

Getting and giving
Are part of life
Sometimes breeds hostility
You can cut with a knife

We wish to get
What we do not have
As long as it's there
On life's book, a tab

But when life has ended
Our struggles are no more
We will reach the state
As into eternity we soar

24. THUS IT IS WRITTEN

Thus it is written
Thus it shall be
The indelible record
For all eternity

Written in stone
Upon the hearts of men
What the future remembers
Is determined by those who win

Losing is not a crime
But those who lose are lost
From the pages of history
This is the ultimate cost

25. GIVE AS YOU ARE GIVEN

Give as you are given
Know as you are known
Do not let your actions
Show you are evil prone

Love others
In all purity be
That in the final judgement
Your motives will be guilt free

When walking the field of life
Let your motives show
Lead others upward
As in all goodness you grow

26. GOOD WILL TO ALL MEN

Good will to all men
To all both small and great
Send out the good will
For unto others do you rate

So do not destroy
But you should build
When your life is over
The future to you will yield

27. NO ONE UNDERSTANDS

No one understands complex things
The whole from the start
But it is simple things we understand
Which of the whole is a part

Complex forces of three or more
Variations that may confuse
Simple forces of one or two
Facts we can use

If you would be understood
Don't confuse the beginners
Keep it simple, stupid
Everyone will understand the winners

28. HAPPINESS IS A STATE OF MIND

Happiness is a state of mind
That leads us to enjoy
For those who have it not
It really does annoy

Happiness is where you are
Your condition you enjoy
You treat the wide world
Like your special toy

Happiness is wanting what you get
Keeping it as your own
Better to be there
Than a king on his throne

29. A SHORT TIME AWAY

A short time away
A little life skipped
Too much bother
Too much been ripped

A little rest
A little sleep
Life passes you by
Evil upon you creep

So plan your work
Work your plan
Success is possible
If you try, you can

30. ON MENTAL STRESS

Mental stress comes from others
Who would your life plan?
They say "Don't grow up
But become a man"

Mental stress comes from within
I want what I cannot have
I search for the answer
As for the future I would grab

Mental stress is from interaction
Of the parts that make the whole
We must prepare ourselves
If this stress doesn't take its toll

31. THINGS WE KNOW

There are things we know
We're finding out more every day
From the very small to the very large
Our knowledge is expanding in every way

But the more we know
Push back the frontiers is our task
The more we find we do not know
The more questions there are to ask

Of our knowledge we may be justly proud
Many mysteries we have solved
But for each question an answer found
Many more are unresolved

But the One who made it all
We can but wonder how
Before His eternal knowledge and power
We must humbly bow

32. THINGS TO DO

Things To Do
Is more than a list
It's work to be performed
It's your job at risk

To do what is required
To stay in touch
Can be overlooked
By those who don't do much

But if you do not do what you should
You will find
Those who you did notice
Will really mind

33. FEW EASY THINGS

Few easy things are important
Few important things are easy
If it were otherwise
Life would be very breezy

If an important thing looks simple
Quick and easy too
You can bet you've missed the point
Your aim has not been true

So don't complain if the way is hard
The path leads ever upward
The goal that you seek
Will offer great reward

34. SOME THINGS ARE REPEATED

Some things are repeated
Over and over again
It is the hope of the speaker
That by repeating they will win

Some things are said but once
But once is more than enough
These spur us into action
Though things are trying and tough

Many things are repeated
By both great and small
Sometimes leading us upward
Saving us from the fall

Listen to what is said
Wisdom can come from every port
Weigh what is said
As through life we sort

35. SOME THINGS A PERSON TASTES

Some things a person tastes but once
Then swallows it whole
But on the bottom line
It's what swallows the person whole

A touch of death
Just a little taste of burn
It sucks you in and swallows
From there, there is no return

The taste of success is sweet
It fills every port
The more we have, the more we want
As life's objectives we sort

But success in what we do
Is the object of our life
A peaceful time to live
A lifetime without strife

Whenever we total up
The good that we do
Let it be judged good
Faithful and true

36. A MORE PERFECT UNION

In order to form a more perfect union
To secure the liberty we enjoy
A constitution was adopted
Three branches the government to deploy

Established so long ago
By men from the upper crust
It gave the common man
A government we can trust

How we kept the union
Was not the easiest thing
The time of testing came
Much dying it did bring

But that time is over
Though we're not in a perfect state
The union has come to be
The nearest to first rate

37. GO TO THE END OF THE WORLD

Go the end of the world
Look over the edge
It is the end of time
The time to turn the page

There will be no tomorrow
Yesterday is but a dream
The all-important now
Life's milk, the cream

So live this day with gusto
For now is all you have
When the morrow comes
An accounting you'll have to give

38. DAYS ARE GROWING SHORT

Days are growing short
The millennium is almost here
We won't have long to worry
Until this time next year

When that day comes
When that day is here
Only God knows
Whether we will cheer

They say the world will stop
No commerce will be
Only time will tell
Only then will we see

39. WHEN YOU'RE YOUNG

When you're young
The world is your cherry
You like to go out
You like to make merry

When you're a little older
You begin to understand
You did what you did
But should have had a reprimand

As you grow into an adult
You acquire responsibility
Understand the bridges you burned
Have become a liability

By the time you became older
Your life was more sedate
Your younger ways
You began to hate

But all in all it is your life
You have lived in a crunch
You pay your money and take your chance
But you only live once

40. WHEN YOU'RE YOUNG II

When you're young
The world is your plum
You can go to the hills
Hunt for gold in the sun

When you're old
Body full of pain
You're caught in a house
You feel insane

What you have done
Is with you all your life
Both the good parts
And those that cause strife

So live for the best
You won't live forever
When you are old
You will regret it never

41. THERE ARE TRUISMS

There are truisms
That are bound within our life
That comes to sit upon our shoulder
Like the edge of a razor knife

The wisdom of a man
Does not upon his education depend
The knowledge that he gets
Gives him a place to begin

The beauty of music
Is not to the volume related
What the volume does for you
Is your hearing degenerated

The value of a painting
Is not in what it represents
But by in large depends
Upon whom the artist was

So when you judge the world
Set your priorities high
Withhold your judgment
When someone offends you draw nigh

42. WHEN YOU'RE YOUNG III

When you're young
The world is young
A new experience everyday
You do your own thing
You make life ring
Someone else must pay

You worry not
You're so hot
You can set the sun on fire
Climb life's poll
With experience untold
No consequences very dire

Then time passes
You see life's messes
As experience you gain
You do your best
To stand the test
As you stand the daily strain

You make do
As through life you go
Much you did spend
The times you've had
Both good and bad
You can never rescind

Then suddenly you're old
You don't feel so bold
As life puts you under strain
You may never know
Where the time did go

You stood in the main

Then life doth end
As it did begin
And you wish to know
That as with life
And all its strife
To what end you must go

43. ONE STANDARD THAT WE MAY HOLD

One standard we may hold
Is taught by someone in the know
To treat others as we would have them
Treat us, this is so

Living in a society or a group
Is not following your nose
It calls for us to live
With discipline as it goes

But does it matter what a man believes?
Or yet a woman too?
It does not affect the facts
But changes what we do

44. BEING POLITICALLY CORRECT

Being politically correct
Is not written into law
Be politically incorrect
Your career will take a yaw

Offend no one
Whether woman, black or red
The repercussions will follow
You will wish that you were dead

Guard your thoughts
Thoughts become a word
You will be sorry
If your thoughts are heard

Follow what I say
Follow this advice
One misplaced word
Negates a lifetime of being nice

45. A SINGLE WORD

A single word
A single thought
From human depth
A message wrought

How deep the message
How long it'll last
Depends upon the hearer
And the hearer's past

How hard the word
How generous the thought
Will be displayed
In actions wrought

46. THE RALLYING CRY

The rallying cry
Where industry is at
Dreaded by employees all
"Cut the fat"

"Cut the fat"
Means many a thing
Don't do anything unnecessary
Unless it has a management ring

No one is ever "the fat"
No thing we want
When management decide to cut
They say need it, they don't

Management looks for ways
To increase their status
By profits increasing
The individual not withstanding

The worker feels sad and lonely
A company is not a friend
But when the worker becomes management
They work to the same end

Don't blame the management
For doing what they do
When you are in their place
You will do the same too

47. WORDS CAN HAVE AN IMMORTAL LIFE

Words can have an immortal life
That lives beyond the pen
They come back to haunt us
Out of the document they're in

When we write or speak
The words of our mind
These sit upon our shoulder
A willing ear to find

Be careful when you speak
Write even less
For at some future time
Your words may cause you distress

48. THERE ARE PRINCIPLES

There are principles
Fitting to be done
By us upon life's stage
Set in stone

To have and to hold
Is not the loss
For nothing of value
Is gotten without cost

For we value things
By the effort we put out
To acquire for ourselves
To help us the future mount

49. LINES ACROSS OUR LIVES

Lines across our lives
Society makes and draws
Lines make us who we are
Defines what we can do

We live best if we know the lines
And do not venture out
For when we cross the lines
We find our motives are in doubt.

50. BODY PAIN

For some pain is a way of life
It fills both body and soul
It can rob the will to live
Makes even the best old

When your body is filled with pain
Your mind becomes distracted
From all the things you like
Your feelings are detracted

But life goes on
And on and on and on
Your life is more important
Then the feeling in your bone

There can be good from everything
Through even what is ill
Been there, done that
You can others with hope fill

So take your life as a lesson
A lesson written on your heart
For in the larger scheme of things
It's important that you do your part

MEET The AUTHOR

Richard Gold has been a Chrisrtian for many years and has been writing Christian poems since 2008.

Gold was born in 1942 in Bartow, Florida, attended college and worked for the Government for 40 years. He is now retired which has given him the time necessary to produce poems, among other things.

Now let us make a list of the advice we have received that made a difference in our lives and keep them for our life and for our children and our children's children.